Wild Violets

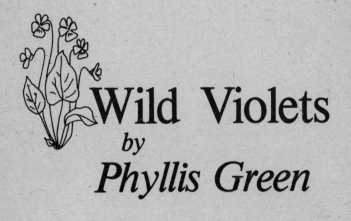

Wild Violets
by
Phyllis Green

A Yearling Book

Published by
Dell Publishing Co., Inc.
1 Dag Hammarskjold Plaza
New York, New York 10017

Yearling ® TM 913705, Dell Publishing Co., Inc.

ISBN: 0-440-49671-3

Reprinted by arrangement with Thomas Nelson, Inc.

Printed in the United States of America

First Yearling printing—June 1980
CW

for my daughter, Sharon

". . . I would give you some violets,
but they withered all when my father died."
—SHAKESPEARE

Wild Violets

Chapter One

In the year 1940 in a small country school called Cranberry Elementary, in upstate New York, the most important person in the fourth grade was a little girl with long dark pigtails. Her name was Cornelia Lee.

Cornelia was only eight and in fourth grade because she had skipped first grade. Cornelia could read with expression, and she was always picked by Teacher (Miss Farmer) to give class thank-you speeches if the class was invited to see the first-grade circus or the fifth-grade science fair.

Most children in the school came from poor families, but Cornelia seemed rich. Her father was an electrician, and he made enough money by wiring and repairing people's houses to allow Cornelia to bring a real lunch-box (not a bag) to school, with a thick peanut-butter sandwich inside it. Her mother also put other items in her lunchbox, which Cornelia didn't always eat, and so she shared them with Grover Wilson, the colored boy who sat behind her.

Cornelia was always dressed the nicest too, because she received hand-me-downs from a cousin in a nearby county who never played rough games. Her cousin liked to read books and play the piano, and she gave her un-torn, unmessed dresses to Cornelia when she outgrew them.

Cornelia was the most important person in the fourth grade, because all the boys who counted said she was their number-one girl friend, and because she could write neater than anybody else in class. Even so, everyone liked Cornelia, and most of the fourth graders wanted to be like her.

But no one wanted to be like Cornelia or to be liked by Cornelia more than a fourth-grade girl who had no friends at all—Ruthie Hickory.

Ruthie was probably the least important person in Miss Farmer's class. And she was surely the poorest and the most funny-looking. She was too poor to have hot water and soap to wash her straight, straw-thick hair, too poor for toothpaste to brush her crooked teeth, too poor even to wear the milky-brown, thick stockings that were held up by garters and that all the other girls hated and tugged at. She was no boy's girl friend. In fact, if a boy looked at her at all it was just to giggle at her, or to whisper, "Here comes Hickory stick," or to hold his nose as she walked by and say, "Gas masks on! Gas masks on!"

Most of the time Ruthie had no lunch to bring to school at all. But she sat too far away from Cornelia for Cornelia to notice and give her some extras. Even De De (Deena) Colona, who one day said all the money her family had was thirteen cents—even De De brought lunch. It was usually toast instead of bread because the Colonas always bought day-old bread.

Ruthie always pretended she was eating so Teacher wouldn't notice and become upset and write notes to her father. She had an old, wrinkled lunch bag she had taken from the wastebasket, and every lunch hour she got it out and put it on her desk and wiggled it around to make everyone think she was eating too. But probably no one noticed because they were all busy talking to their friends as they ate, and Ruthie had no friends.

Ruthie would wiggle her bag as Cornelia took out all the extra things from her lunch box and pass them back to Grover. Sometimes she could hear some of the things Cornelia would say to the children who sat near her, and Ruthie would pretend Cornelia was talking just to her.

Cornelia had been to Lake Chautauqua in the summer

for a whole month with her grandparents. And she had almost been chosen to lead the children's orchestra. Actually, she *had* been chosen, but somebody important with a daughter in the group had decided *his* daughter should lead the orchestra, so Cornelia was told she couldn't do it. Everyone moaned when they heard that. Ruthie felt terrible for Cornelia. She knew Cornelia would have been the best orchestra leader.

Then Cornelia told of finding fossils at Lake Chautauqua and a locust shell and about swimming lessons and about how she could jump right into the seaweed and it didn't bother her and of how she almost drowned during her swimming test and how she had for the first time in her life smelled the breath of someone who had been eating onions and it "stunk." Cornelia had had an exciting summer, Ruthie thought.

Ruthie even lived in the same direction as Cornelia, only Ruthie lived a few hills beyond. But she never walked home from school with Cornelia. Cornelia usually walked home with Mercy Berry, another fourth grader, who was chubby, blond, and round-faced, and who had a habit of hitting you, even if you were a friend. Every time Mercy said something she'd reach out and bang somebody's back or arm. She always thought she was funny, too. Ruthie didn't know why Cornelia liked Mercy, except that she knew Cornelia liked everybody. Ruthie thought, Cornelia would even like me if she knew I existed.

Another person Cornelia walked home with, and he

carried her books, was Edgar Miller from the fifth grade. Edgar had told everyone, when he was in third grade and Cornelia in second, that she was his girl friend. So some days he'd take her books and walk her home, and Ruthie would follow them. She thought it was funny that Edgar and Cornelia never talked. Cornelia found enough to talk about with everyone else, but with Edgar she was speechless and shy.

After Ruthie passed Cornelia's house, she would walk on, over several more hills, to hers. She was glad she lived farthest from the school because this way no one could see what she called home. It was an old black barn in the middle of a field. Her father had tried to put rooms in the barn and in so doing had proved he was not a carpenter. It wasn't a pretty barn. It was just a weathered, broken-down sort of barn, and was nothing like Cornelia's white two-bedroom bungalow. To Ruthie, Cornelia's house looked almost like a small castle.

Sometimes Ruthie's mother would be home and sometimes she wouldn't. Sometimes she was away for weeks at a time. But Ruthie's father was always home by dark. She could count on that. And together they would try to scramble together some odds and ends for their dinner. They usually had a potato each, perhaps an apple from a nearby orchard, and a cup of soup. If her father had found some odd jobs to do that day and gotten paid for it, they would have an egg as a special treat. And when Mr. Hickory shot a rabbit, dinner was a feast.

Along with the barn, Ruthie's father had a piece of

rocky, hilly land that wasn't any good for farming. He had bought it as farming land before the Depression, but then, after spending all his money on it, had found he couldn't farm it and couldn't sell it. He had been doing odd jobs ever since.

Ruthie had been born in 1931, and she had always lived in the barn and in poverty.

Chapter Two

Ruthie usually felt herself on the outside of everything that happened in the fourth grade at Cranberry School. She wasn't even one of the girls who were embarrassed by Miss Farmer in the lipstick incident. Most of the girls—and Cornelia was right in there with them—wore lipstick to school one day. Ruthie supposed they had planned it that way, but she as usual had not been in on the planning, or she would have done it too. Her mother usually had some lipstick lying around, whether she was home or not.

15

When Miss Farmer spotted the girls with their bright-red lips she had looked horrified. She had immediately stopped roll call and given a long speech on girls who were too young to wear lipstick and on how they would be thought of as hussies. Then she passed out the rough, yellow paper towels and lined the girls up to go down to the washroom to scrub off their ruby lips. Ruthie was scared for the girls and thought poor Cornelia might cry. But the long pigtails were flipping as Cornelia turned her head and brazenly smiled and winked at the class on her way to the washroom. How Ruthie longed to be punished with them. Everything Cornelia did turned out to be the right thing to do, even when it was wrong.

In November, Ruthie and most of the rest of the class whose parents were Democrats felt like winners when President Roosevelt won the election. But Cornelia, who was Republican, started telling them about her new puppy, which she had named Willkie after Roosevelt's opponent, and she told them how she had wanted to stay up to listen to the radio and hear if Willkie won.

But Cornelia's father wouldn't let her stay up that late. He promised her that when she woke up in the morning, Willkie would have won. Everyone felt sorry that dear Cornelia had been disappointed. But they really felt awful the next month when the puppy, Willkie, got sick and died. It was from a terrible dog disease, distemper, and Cornelia's parents told her they would not be allowed to get another dog for a whole year, for fear the new dog would catch the distemper too.

When they heard about the puppy Willkie dying, every Democratic fourth grader hung his head in shame to think that his parents had voted for Roosevelt.

At Christmastime, Miss Farmer let the fourth graders put on a play that they had written themselves. Of course Cornelia played the lead role of Mrs. Stevens. The play was called "Mrs. Stevens' Strange Christmas Party." It was about a rich lady, Mrs. Stevens, who decided to give a party for a group of orphans. She had hired a man to dress up and play Santa Claus and he was to come down her chimney during the party. But the pretend Santa Claus got stuck in the chimney because he was fat to begin with, and to everyone's surprise, the *real* Santa Claus, direct from the North Pole, showed up at the party by walking through the front door. The play was very funny, especially the part where Harry Tompkins, who played the pretend Santa, got stuck in the chimney.

Even Ruthie had a part in the play. She was Mrs. Stevens' maid. And Grover Wilson was to be the butler, but he misunderstood and came to dress rehearsal with a pink maid's costume (it was one of his mother's, who was a maid). Everyone got a laugh out of the two maids, except Ruthie, who felt her part had been diminished when Grover took over and made everyone laugh.

They gave the play for the other grades at Cranberry

and everyone laughed and applauded, but they applauded most of all for Cornelia. Some of the girls thought Cornelia should become a movie star in Hollywood when she grew up and Cornelia admitted she was thinking about it.

Chapter Three

Ruthie's mother came home from wherever she had been in time for Christmas but not in time to see the play. Cornelia's mother, of course, came to the play. She came to every school event and also to the Mother's Club. Ruthie often wished her own mother would be more like Mrs. Lee.

Ruthie's mother would come and go like a summer storm. One minute she was there and the next minute she wasn't. Ruthie would hear her say those familiar words, "I can't take it any longer," and soon she would pack a bag and be off to wherever it was she went. It was a big mystery to Ruthie. Where did you go when you couldn't take it any longer? Ruthie didn't know, and deep down inside, she didn't want to know. She played at imagining her mother to be a fairy princess who sometimes got fed up with being human and went back home to live with her king and queen fairy parents.

This time at Christmas when her mother came home, she brought presents. For Ruthie there was a pink ruffled rayon party dress that looked almost new. Ruthie pretended it was a discarded fairy party dress, and she couldn't wait for school to begin after the New Year so she could wear it. Maybe Cornelia would like it. Maybe she would want to borrow it for a party she might be invited to. Ruthie hoped no one would see the grease mark on the hem in the back, and that no one would notice that she smelled when they saw the pretty party dress. It was probably a magic dress besides, and would make her lots of friends.

At least, if someone asked her what she got for Christmas, she could smile and say, "Why, this beautiful party dress." It wasn't possible to tell people that her father's sister, Aunt Lenore, always sent her two pairs of underpants. Her parents got a fruitcake from Aunt Lenore and Uncle Bob for Christmas. Ruthie ate all the nuts because that was the only part she liked.

When Ruthie's mother was home she spent a great deal of time curling her hair and putting on and taking off nail polish. Sometimes she was home only a week or two before she took off again to "somewhere." But once she was home for a whole year. Ruthie was always careful to be helpful and good when her mother was home. She never wanted to give her reason to leave.

Once Ruthie had begged, "Take me with you."

Her mother had laughed gently and bent down to kiss her. "Honey, your daddy needs you here to take care of him. Be a big girl now and don't cry. I'll be seeing you soon."

So Ruthie and her father would be alone again. When he got home from looking for odd jobs he never mentioned that Ruthie's mother had run off again. But he seemed to be especially kind to Ruthie for a few days after that. And in time they both sort of got used to Ruthie's mother's running in and out.

But though Ruthie would never say so, it mattered to her that hers was not a real family, like the Lees, for instance, with a mother who stayed home and packed big lunches for her little girl to take to school. She wished her mother would braid her hair like Cornelia's, too. But her mother said it was too short and she couldn't do a thing with it, couldn't even braid it.

And Ruthie knew she smelled. But she had no soap, and only cold water. There was just so much you could do to get clean with cold water. She heard the boys say their mischievous "Gas masks on!" and her heart wept. It was her secret dream to have a bathroom with a big tub and lots of hot water and good-smelling bubbles and perfumes. But in the meantime, before her dream would come true, all she had was the pump outside and her gray-tinted skin.

Sometimes in the very depth of winter she was allowed to use the stove to heat some bath water, but the warmth of the stove cost her father precious pennies. Warm water was extremely rare for Ruthie. Soap was something she could not remember ever having. So she washed her hands extra hard at school with the slimy green liquid soap in the girl's washroom.

Chapter Four

Cornelia had been back to school only four days in January when she became sick with scarlet fever. She was home sick a whole month.

One day, in art class, everyone made a get-well card for Cornelia. Ruthie put a sad cat on hers and wrote, "This cat will be sad until you get back to school, and I will too." She wished she could draw better so hers would be the prettiest and Cornelia's favorite.

Everyone missed Cornelia. Harry Tompkins and his mother stopped by one day after school with a quart of ice cream for Cornelia. Ruthie watched them take it inside the Lees' house, and all the way home she wondered what flavor it was. She herself had had a strawberry cone once and it had been delicious.

Soon after Harry Tompkins and his mother took ice cream to Cornelia, a rumor went around Cranberry that Edgar Miller was upset. Ruthie heard he had had a fight with Harry about the whole thing and that Harry's nose had been bloodied, even though he said the whole thing had been his mother's idea.

The next Sunday after church Edgar stayed to talk to the minister. He said he knew a sick person, and that he would appreciate it if the minister would let him take the basket of church flowers to this person. The minister said he could. So Edgar picked up the large green wicker basket of white carnations and pink gladioli and delivered it at Cornelia's door.

Lots of fourth graders were sick that January with scarlet fever or chicken pox or measles. Mr. Hickory told Ruthie she had better not get sick because he couldn't afford any fool doctor. So she concentrated hard on staying well and made it to school every day, even the day it snowed fourteen inches and there were five-foot drifts in the hills.

Cornelia got better and was back to school in time for the Valentine party.

The whole room was decorated with red and white hearts. Streamers and chains of red and white went from the teacher's desk to the top of the blackboard. Miss Farmer had written "Happy Valentine's Day" on the blackboard in big chalk letters. Out of a big cardboard box, the class had made a red-and-white house with hearts for windows and doors. There was a slot in the roof and for several days the children had been bringing in valentine cards and pushing them into the slot. The Valentine House would be opened during the party and the valentines passed out.

Edgar Miller had come into the fourth grade before school started and put a few cards in the slot. He also had another card, but it was too big for the slot. So he laid it beside the Valentine House. The children took turns peeking at the name on it. Who was getting a big card? Grover Wilson measured it with his ruler. He said it was twelve inches long and nine inches wide. When Ruthie peeked at the card she saw that it was for Cornelia.

Ruthie's father had thought he could give her some money to buy some valentines, but he finally said he couldn't. Well, she thought, I don't know why I'm so disappointed. It's no different from other years. I guess anyone would faint if they got a real card from me. But she took a piece of lined school paper and drew a heart on it and colored it red. She printed "Be My Valentine. Ruthie H." on it. Then she folded it up, wrote "Cornelia" on the front, and slid it into the Valentine House.

Ruthie was glad Cornelia was back in time for the party. Cornelia always liked parties. And Cornelia always got a whole pile of valentines and set the whole class crazy with laughing at the way she read them aloud. Ruthie remembered that last year, in third grade, Cornelia received thirty-seven valentines. The nearest amount to that was twenty for the third-grade teacher. Ruthie had received two valentines last year, one from Cornelia, who brought a card for each child in the class, and one from the teacher, Mrs. Bennington.

When the party started everyone received a white cupcake with white icing and a little red cinnamon heart on top from Miss Farmer. And on a paper plate everyone got a slice of brick ice cream with vanilla and raspberry and pineapple strips. Ruthie cut it and ate it carefully with the flat wooden spoon, one color at a time, so she wouldn't get the flavors mixed up or waste a drop.

When Miss Farmer opened the Valentine House, everyone got excited. Grover and Harry were postmen. Miss Farmer called out the names on the envelopes, and they passed them out. Everyone grew quiet listening for his own name. When Mercy Berry heard her name on the first card, she screamed. All the girls giggled, then got quiet again so they'd hear their names being called. Ruthie didn't look at Miss Farmer. She didn't even listen. She was trying hard to daydream and keep out the party sounds, but every once in a while she would look at Cornelia's desk to see how the cards were piling up and to see if Cornelia had received her card yet.

The big envelope was on Cornelia's desk, but she was not opening it. "Why don't you open it?" De De asked.

Cornelia looked embarrassed and shoved it under the others, trying to pretend it wasn't there. "I don't want to open it till I get home."

De De said, "Cornelia! Your face is as red as a valentine!"

Ruthie wanted to say something mean to De De. Poor Cornelia looked as if she might cry. Ruthie put her hands over her mouth, so no one could see, and secretly stuck her tongue out at De De Colona.

Miss Farmer said, "Ruthie Hickory!"

Ruthie wanted to die. But then she realized that Miss Farmer was calling out her name for a valentine. A valentine! Her first this year! Harry delivered it to her. Actually, he threw it on her desk from ten feet away. But she didn't care. She picked it up and looked at it. Yes. That was her name all right. It was written so neatly, too. She opened it carefully and a red lollipop fell out. She read the card. It was from Miss Farmer. Ruthie smiled. She held the lollipop. I'm going to save it for Daddy, she thought. She put it in her pocket, the one that didn't have a hole in it.

And then she couldn't believe it. The teacher called her name again, and then *again*. Two in a row! Everyone turned to look at her. And she had a big party smile on her face. One card was from Cornelia. It had a white pony on it. The other card wasn't signed, except to say, "Your Secret Pal." Ruthie thought it was really mysterious. Who could have sent it? It was very neat writing, about as neat as Miss Farmer's. It was very exciting to wonder who her secret pal was.

Ruthie didn't get any more valentines, but she didn't care. She would take these home and show them to her father and tell him all about the wonderful party.

Chapter Five

In March, Cornelia and Mercy and De De started a club. They put a notice on the bulletin board that any fourth-grade girl could belong. It was going to be a book club, because Cornelia's and Mercy's mothers both belonged to the ladies' book club. It would even be called Book Club and whoever's turn it was would read a book and give a five-minute report on it, and then refreshments would be served.

Ruthie liked the sound of it. Any fourth-grade girl could join! And she was certainly a fourth-grade girl.

The first meeting was to be at Cornelia's house. It would be the opening meeting, with the election of officers.

The Book Club met in Cornelia's bedroom. Five girls attended the first meeting: Cornelia, Mercy Berry, De De Colona, Lucy Lincoln (who had just moved into the house next to De De and was also in fourth grade), and Ruthie.

Cornelia called the meeting to order because it was her club and her house and her idea.

"We'll now have nominations for president," she said.

De De raised her hand. "I nominate Cornelia Lee."

"Anyone else?" Cornelia asked.

Mercy started to giggle. "I nominate Ruthie Hickory."

The other girls smiled and Ruthie did too. Nominated for president! That was something.

Cornelia and Ruthie had to close their eyes for the vote. Mercy called out, "Who wants Cornelia?"

Ruthie and Mercy, De De and Lucy raised their hands.

"Who wants Ruthie?" she asked.

Cornelia raised her hand. Mercy announced, "You're president, Cornelia."

Ruthie was nominated for vice president, too, along with De De Colona. De De got five votes because she voted for herself.

Nominations for treasurer were next. Mercy Berry was nominated, and so was Ruthie. Mercy got four votes. Cornelia voted for Ruthie for treasurer.

The last office was Secretary. De De nominated Lucy Lincoln. Mercy nominated Ruthie. But Ruthie was getting to feel funny about being nominated so much and not getting elected. She didn't know why. She thought she should be happy to be nominated. But she had a strange feeling, hard to define.

"I don't really want to be secretary. Thank you just the same," she said.

"Are you sure?" Cornelia asked.

"Well," Mercy said, "looks like you're secretary, Lucy!"

Mercy decided, as treasurer, that everyone should bring a nickel dues every week. Ruthie felt sick, and it must have shown on her face. Cornelia kicked Mercy and said that, as president, she had the final say.

"You don't *have* to bring a nickel. That's not the rule. The rule is if you *want* to bring a nickel. If you *feel* like bringing a nickel, then Mercy will collect it. But if you forget or plain just don't feel like bringing a nickel, then you don't."

Before refreshments were served (real Oreo cookies from the grocery store), Cornelia told Lucy that she was to read a book and report on it at the next meeting.

"Can it be one I've already read?"

Nobody seemed to know the answer to that. So they let Lucy decide.

"Okay, I'll do *Heidi*."

Everyone screamed at her. "You're not supposed to tell ahead of time!"

Mercy said, "Not that old thing. I already read it."

"Okay," Lucy said, "I'll do another one. A surprise."

The Book Club met every week for three months. Then school was out for the summer and the club broke up. In those three months, Mercy had collected $1.35. No one ever saw the money again. Ruthie heard that Cornelia and De De had gone over to Mercy's house during the summer and told her she had to give the money back. But she hit them with a big stick and chased them off her property.

Chapter Six

In the summer, when she came home, Ruthie's mother had taken up smoking. She had taken to smoking all day long. When one cigarette was finished, she quick lit up another, so her fingers wouldn't get that empty feeling. She smoked sitting up and she smoked lying down. She could even smoke while polishing her fingernails and not make one smear.

One night in the beginning of July, a hot, muggy, hard-to-get-to-sleep night, she was smoking in bed. Her and Ruthie's father's bed was up in what used to be the hayloft. Ruthie slept on the couch in the main room. The night was the seventh of July, 1941. The ashes got real long on her cigarette and started falling off onto the sheet as she smoked, her eyes closed. She fell asleep and the cigarette fell from her fingers. It just smoked on by itself for a while and then a black hole burned in the sheet. Pretty soon there was a small fire, which started to spread. When Ruthie's father woke up, one whole edge of the bed was on fire.

He started yelling for Ruthie to get out of the house and for her mother to wake up. He grabbed his shoe and tried to pound out the flames. But they were too high. He helped his wife down the steps from the loft. They grabbed Ruthie and ran outside.

Mr. Hickory ran over the hill to get help. The volunteer fire company was called, and soon sirens were screaming and bells were ringing. A big red fire truck drove onto the Hickorys' dirt road and up the hill to put out the fire in their home.

Flames were shooting out the roof of the loft as Ruthie and her mother stood under the one tree on the hill staring at the fire. Her mother was shaking and making sounds that seemed to say *Nnahn-shas*. It was a moan or a quiet scream. Ruthie hugged her mother and looked at her. The light from the fire cast a red glow on her skin. She didn't seem to be crying, though, because no tears were coming out of her eyes, but Ruthie thought the sounds were sort of crying sounds.

"You won't catch me crying," her mother said when

she caught her breath. "I can't cry anymore. No tears come."

Ruthie patted her mother's back. "It'll be all right, Mom. The firemen are here now."

Her mother said, "I cried once, when I was about your age. Nobody ever cried that hard. I used up all my tears. And I've been dry ever since. It was when my daddy died, right here" —she held out her arms— "right here in my arms. I was only ten years old and I cried enough for a lifetime."

"I'm ten now. I turned ten when you were away," Ruthie said.

"Did you now? Well, the time slipped by me. I was ten and now you're ten. We were the same age, then."

Ruthie nodded even though it confused her.

"No one will ever see me cry again," her mother said. "Never."

The volunteer firemen were running around and yelling about hoses and water. Ruthie thought she saw Cornelia's father, Mr. Lee. He was fire chief, so she probably did see him.

Mr. Hickory had run back into the house and brought out a cardboard box of clothes. Ruthie hoped he had saved her pink party dress. It was in a Heinz 57 Varieties box with her other things.

He brought out a box that looked like her mother's. Mrs. Hickory ran over to the box and found a pale-blue silk robe to throw around her nightgown. "This is better.

I felt practically naked out here with all those firemen around. How about you, Ruthie? You want to put on this dress of mine over your pajamas?" Ruthie put on her mother's yellow dress. It almost fit. She'd *thought* she was nearly as tall as her mother.

The flames seemed to be slowing down, but there was black smoke everywhere. It made Ruthie cough and choke. Finally Mr. Lee told the men to shut down the hoses. The fire was out.

It was almost five o'clock in the morning. The sky was growing light. And for the first time Ruthie looked back at the dirt road and saw all the cars parked there. People were standing against their cars. They had been watching her fire. For how long? she wondered. She saw some children from the school with their parents. She saw Cornelia and Mrs. Lee! Just about everyone had come to see her old barn of a house burn down. She wanted to die. Now everyone knew what an awful place she lived in. Now they knew she was the poorest one of all.

Mr. Hickory ran around shaking all the firemen's hands and thanking them. Ruthie's mother walked around the outside of the barn, saying, "What are we going to do? This place is a mess."

Finally all the people and the firemen left. Ruthie looked at her mother and father.

"Well," her father said, "we were lucky. We have half a house. It's better than none."

"I'll bet it stinks," her mother said.

"We'll rebuild," her father said.

36

"With what? You're a real dreamer, Tommy. Just what do you think they're doing? Giving wood away?"

"Help me get the furniture out to air. The furniture that's left," he said.

"I'll help!" Ruthie said.

She helped her father all morning while her mother walked around wringing her hands and saying, "You're crazy, Tommy, to try and save this junk. I don't see how you can take it. I can't stand looking at this mess."

By the afternoon, the part of the barn that was left had been cleaned out and aired. Mr. Hickory said Ruthie had to take a nap because she had worked so hard. She lay down on the still smoky-smelling couch and went right to sleep.

When she woke up a few hours later, she saw her father watching her.

"Did she go yet?" she asked him.

"Not yet. She's sitting out by the tree," he said.

Ruthie ran to her father and hugged him. "Can I go down to the creek awhile? I'll come home when she's gone. I don't want to hear her say it."

Her father nodded. "When it starts to get dark, you come home lickety-split," he said. "Wait!" He put two slices of bread in her hand. "Here, have a picnic."

Ruthie ran down to her favorite place by the creek. She ate her bread and searched for polliwogs.

Several days later the Catholic priest came by and talked to her father. He said a local lumber store wanted to donate some wood to the church. He looked at Ruthie and said it was a shame a fine girl like Ruthie wasn't getting any religious education.

It seemed like a fair exchange to Mr. Hickory. So he got the wood to rebuild their house, and for a few months that summer Ruthie was a Catholic.

Chapter Seven

The invitations to Cornelia's birthday party were cut in the shape of clowns. Their costumes were made of purple-and-white checks, and they had red bushy hair. Ruthie slept with her invitation under her pillow for a week before the party, till the clown became torn and ragged and the ink was so smeared that she could hardly read the date. It didn't matter. She knew it by heart. August 20, 1941. Three o'clock in the afternoon.

Her father had given her a dime to buy a present for

Cornelia. She had picked out two beautiful light-blue barrettes for Cornelia to wear in her hair. She wrapped the barrettes as neatly as she could in white tissue paper and tied the package with some green string her father had saved.

At ten minutes to three all eleven girls in Cornelia's class at Cranberry started descending on the Lee house. They all wore their best dresses and all carried a small gift. Cornelia had a big smile on her face as she opened the door to let them in.

And Mrs. Lee knew how to give a good party. There was pink everywhere! Pink balloons hanging from the ceiling, pink crepe paper decorating the doorways. And Cornelia, the birthday girl, wore a puffy pink dress and pink silk ribbons on each long braid.

First they all sat in a circle on the living-room rug while Cornelia opened the gifts. Mercy Berry gave her a Mickey Mouse coloring book and crayons. De De Colona's gift was a small box of chocolate candy. As soon as Cornelia had opened Ruthie's present, she took the blue barrettes off the white cardboard and clipped them in her hair, one above each ear. Everyone said they looked real pretty, too. It made Ruthie feel good. Cornelia also received a paper-doll book, a domino game, silk plaid ribbons for her hair, a pair of white socks, an American flag pin, which she put on her puffy pink dress, white angora yarn and knitting needles, a box of colored drawing pencils, and modeling clay. Cornelia was very sweet about thanking each girl for her gift.

Then she showed them her birthday present from her mother and father.

It was a ring. A real ring! The band was real gold. And the soft-blue stone was set up high on gold prongs.

"It's a turquoise stone," Cornelia said.

The girls oohed and aahed over the beauty of the ring, and some moaned that it was not theirs. But Ruthie thought it was right for Cornelia to have it. Cornelia was more like a princess than an ordinary girl. And princesses were expected to have nice things.

The ring, it turned out, had been Mrs. Lee's when she was a little girl. And before that, it had belonged to Cornelia's grandmother, who had worn it when she was a girl.

Then Mrs. Lee called the girls to the dining room, where a huge cake with pink icing stood in the center of the table. The cake was white inside and so creamy and delicious. The ice cream served with it was strawberry. Ruthie licked her lips. Small round pink mints had been placed on each girl's plate. And everyone had a glass of milk.

After eating, it was games! Button . . . Button, Who's Got the Button? and BlindMan's Buff. They went outside to play Mother, May I? and Red Light—Green Light. Soon the girls were playing anything they wanted and some were running through the vacant lot next to Cornelia's house. It was a giggling time and a fun party.

Suddenly Cornelia stopped running and looked down at her right hand. The ring! Something was wrong. She stared at the ring. The gold band was there and the long strong prongs. But the little blue turquoise stone was gone.

She started to cry and started running here and there looking for the stone. Frightened, desperate sounds were coming from her throat, and big tears fell onto the pink dress. The other girls ran to Cornelia to see what was the matter.

"My ring!" she managed to say.

They all looked at her ring. Their eyes became very large as they stared at the empty gold prongs. Nobody spoke. Rings are special things for girls, and the missing stone frightened them all.

Finally someone said, "Let's look for it! I bet we can find it."

They walked carefully through the vacant lot, each girl straining to see a small blue turquoise stone lying perhaps on a leaf, or beside a twig, or at the root of a bramble. They began looking with much hope and enthusiasm. But after searching for almost an hour, they were beginning to tire and became convinced it was hopeless.

Finally Cornelia, her shoulders slumped, had to go into the house and show her mother what had happened to the ring.

Chapter Eight

Mrs. Lee asked all the girls to sit down in the living room. Cornelia sat beside her mother and laid her head in her lap.

"I want to tell you a story," Mrs. Lee said. "It's about three little girls and one ring."

Everyone looked surprised. A story about a ring when Cornelia was so sad about losing the little turquoise stone?

Mrs. Lee patted Cornelia's back and told the story.

"Fifty years ago on a Christmas Day, a little girl named

Maudie received a lovely ring as a present. It was a gold ring. Real gold. And the prongs rose up to clasp a lovely turquoise-blue stone. Maudie loved her Christmas ring. She wore it every day. She swore she'd never take it off.

"But the next summer her best friend took ill. The friend had to stay in bed for two months, and Maudie was not allowed to visit her for fear she would get the terrible illness herself. The lonely weeks went by. Maudie had no one to play with, so she took to playing games with her ring. She would sit out under an old oak tree on her large front lawn. She would take off the ring and hide it in the knots of the tree or in the dirt around its bulging roots. Then she would close her eyes and turn around and around until she was dizzy. When she opened her eyes, bushes swayed, houses moved and melted, everything was streaking in whirling circles. Finally Maudie was so dizzy that she would fall to the ground. When she got over her dizziness she would go back to the tree and try to remember where she had hidden her ring. It was a foolish thing to do, but remember, she was a little girl trying to find a game to pass the lonely hours.

"Luckily for Maudie, she never *lost* the ring for long, though once, she thought for sure she couldn't find the root she had hidden it under.

"When Maudie grew up to be a woman, she had a daughter of her own. She named her Alice. When Alice was nine years old, she found a lovely ring in her Easter basket. It was on top of a chocolate egg. The ring was gold. Yes. Real gold. And I think you know it had a pretty turquoise-blue stone set on long gold prongs. Alice also loved the ring. She thought it was the most beautiful ring in the whole world. One day Alice was playing with some girl friends. One of them got the idea of throwing the ring with her eyes closed. The first one to find it in the tall grass would win the game. They thought the game was exciting. But once, when Alice threw it, no one found it. They crawled around, searching through the grass, but the ring was lost.

"Alice told her mother. But what could her mother say? For she was Maudie, who had played dangerous games herself with the same ring. The ring was missing for five days. Then Alice's father saw it when he was mowing the lawn. It was slightly bent out of shape, but he managed to straighten it so it would fit Alice's finger once more. Alice promised not to be so careless again with such a precious possession. But the ring became lost, no one knew how, for three weeks when she was eleven. It turned out to have fallen down the bathroom-sink drain. The plumber who came to unclog the sink found it.

"When Alice grew up to be a woman, she also had a daughter. She called her little girl Cornelia. For Cornelia's ninth birthday party, she invited the girls in her class at school. They all came dressed so prettily and bringing lovely, thoughtful gifts for Cornelia. Cornelia showed them her birthday ring—a lovely gold ring, holding a softly colored blue stone in its upturned prongs. While

45

playing games, the blue stone escaped from the prongs. The girls searched and searched for it, but it was too small to be found.

"Well, that is the story so far," Mrs. Lee said, "but the story is far from finished. The little gold ring is very old and has had many adventures. I think it is an enchanted ring that can never really be lost for long. The little blue stone will turn up when we least expect it. So don't feel sad, girls, nor you, Cornelia. I know, or my name isn't Alice, that the turquoise stone will be found again."

The girls smiled and felt better. Cornelia passed out a birthday favor to each of them. It was a jump rope. They all tried out their jump ropes as they skipped and jumped home, thinking Cornelia's party had been the best party they had ever been to.

Chapter Nine

When Ruthie, Cornelia, and the others started back to school in September, 1941, there was talk about war. Their parents whispered about war and Germans and bombs on London. It all sounded very frightening but also far away. There was even talk of another war, on the other side of the world, between the Japanese and Chinese peoples. The boys in the fifth-grade class at Cranberry thought war was exciting, and they practiced shooting pretend guns and cannons at each other during lunch recess. The girls played softball and hide and seek.

There was a new music teacher at Cranberry that fall. Her name was Miss Willipie, but the boys called her Miss Whippoorwill. They said she even looked like a bird. The fifth-grade class had music twice a week with Miss Willipie, and nobody liked it very much. They had to learn every new song by singing "Loo—loo—loo" instead of the words. They felt all they ever did was "Loo—loo—loo," and it got to be a huge joke.

"Here comes Loo—Loo Whippoorwill," Grover Wilson would say when Miss Willipie walked into the fifth-grade class.

Everyone would giggle, and Miss Willipie would shake her long blond curls and screw her face up all tight and nervous.

Everyone had wanted to ask, but finally Harry Tompkins got the courage. He raised his hand.

Miss Willipie nodded for him to speak.

"Is your boyfriend named Louie? Is that why we have to sing 'Loo—loo—loo' all the time?"

The whole class was breathlessly quiet.

Miss Willipie stared at all of them. Then she picked up her books and ran out of the room crying.

"What's the matter with her?" Harry said. "I only asked a simple question."

Some of the boys grinned halfheartedly, but mostly, everyone felt uncomfortable.

Fifth grade seemed different to Ruthie, and not only because it was a graduation to the second floor of Cranberry School. That was important, of course, to get away from the babies of the school and to get upstairs with the big kids. But fifth grade was different. Maybe it was all the talk and whispering about war. Maybe it was the teacher, Mrs. Krauss, who seemed so much stricter than Miss Farmer had been. Maybe it was because arithmetic was getting so hard now, with fractions and decimals and long division. Maybe it was because Ruthie had thought that being in the Book Club last year and being invited to Cornelia's birthday party would make her have friends this year, when it really didn't make any difference at all. And the boys might have forgotten their multiplication tables over the summer, but they didn't forget to say "Gas masks on" whenever Ruthie walked by.

One day when Grover Wilson was absent, Mrs. Krauss asked the children to turn back to a story in their reading books that they had skipped before. It was a story of a colored boy who was hoping to get a bicycle for his birthday. There were a lot of "sho' 'nuffs" and "yes'ms" in the story.

Mrs. Krauss asked Cornelia to read the part of the colored boy and the rest of the class took turns on the other parts. Cornelia was amazing. She sounded just like Grover as she read the lines. Ruthie thought if she closed her eyes, she would absolutely believe it was Grover. It just went to prove that Cornelia would be a fine actress someday and live in a big house in Hollywood and have tons of boyfriends.

And somehow no one mentioned to Grover, when he came back to school, that they had read *that* story.

On December 7, 1941, the Japanese made their attack on Pearl Harbor. Pearl Harbor was the American Navy base in Hawaii. The Japanese surprised the Americans at dawn and sank or damaged 8 big battleships, destroyed 188 airplanes, and killed over 2,000 men. President Roosevelt then declared war against both the Japanese and Germans (who had conquered most of Europe and were now bombing England, a country friendly to America).

Now all the war talk was out in the open. Men would be soldiers, and in the spring Victory gardens would be planted. Everyone talked about "Japs" and "Nazis," about Hitler and Mussolini. Mercy Berry even said Mrs. Krauss was a "Nazi" because her husband had been born in Germany and spoke with an accent. Ruthie thought it was a scary time, with boys on the playground shouting "Kill the bloody Japs," and putting a finger under their nose (for a moustache like Hitler had) and pulling their hair down onto their forehead and raising their right arm and screaming *"Heil Hitler,"* which was the Nazi salute.

And Ruthie's mother wasn't home. She hadn't been home for a long time.

One night, near Christmas, her father let her stay up late so she could finish a book she had brought home from the school library. When she finally closed the book, tears were running out of her eyes.

Her father looked at her. He smiled. "Some sad story, huh?" he asked.

Ruthie shook her head.

"Then why the tears?" he asked. He patted his knee, which meant for her to come sit on it.

She slowly walked over to him. She was ten now, ten and a half, really, and she felt like a baby sitting on her father's knee. Still she got up on it, and his arm on her shoulder felt good.

"What's the matter, Ruthie?" he said.

Ruthie sighed. "When's she coming back? It's almost Christmas. I don't think she's ever coming back again."

"Listen, it doesn't matter. We're going to have Christmas anyhow. I want you to go buy yourself some of those pretty blue barrettes like the ones you gave the Lee girl for her birthday."

"Where does she go when she goes?" Ruthie pleaded.

Her father didn't answer.

"Daddy, are you going to be a soldier?"

"I might be called."

"Then what will I do?"

Mr. Hickory kissed her forehead. "If it happens, you'll be taken good care of. Don't worry about that. Now, it's real late. I want you to go right to bed."

Chapter Ten

One day in March, 1942, Ruthie walked out of school and saw Cornelia sitting on the front stone steps. She was looking down and kicking at pebbles by her feet. Ruthie stopped at the top of the steps, trying to think of something nice to say to Cornelia.

Cornelia's father was very ill. And Edgar Miller, her special friend, was moving away to New Mexico. Cornelia had been unusually quiet the last few weeks. She never laughed and almost never smiled. It just wasn't like Cornelia.

But Ruthie couldn't think of anything to say.

Edgar Miller came out of the school and took Cornelia's books. They started walking home.

Ruthie slowly followed, not too near, not too far, not actually listening to their conversation, but they weren't whispering and the sounds sort of zoomed back to her ears. It was surprising. Cornelia and Edgar usually never talked, but this day they talked and talked.

"You can't believe all the boxes around our house," Edgar said.

"I hear there's a lot of desert in New Mexico," Cornelia said.

"Yeah."

"I bet you'll like it."

"I might get a pony when we get out there."

Cornelia turned her head so fast that her pigtails flipped and she tripped over a small stone. "Edgar! A pony, that's great!" she said.

Edgar looked at Cornelia and smiled.

"Your father's real smart, isn't he?" Cornelia asked.

Edgar shrugged his shoulders. "I guess so," he said.

"I hope he likes his new job. It's a secret job, isn't it?"

"It might be a government job. But I don't know."

They turned onto the tarred road where Cornelia lived.

"How's your dad doing?" Edgar asked.

A choking sound came from Cornelia's throat.

"You don't have to talk about it," Edgar said.

Cornelia wiped her eyes. "That's okay. I can talk about it. He's still awful sick."

"When will he come home from the hospital?"

"We don't know," Cornelia whispered.

They were at Cornelia's driveway.

"Well," Edgar said, and handed her her books. "Well, I'll walk you home until we leave. That's three more days."

"Okay," Cornelia said. " 'Bye."

Edgar waved and walked backward a few steps, almost bumping into Ruthie. Then he turned and walked down the hill to his house.

"Hi," Ruthie said.

Cornelia was still waving to Edgar. She seemed very far away in her thoughts, as far away as New Mexico, Ruthie thought.

"Hi," Ruthie said again.

"Oh, hi, Ruthie," Cornelia said.

Ruthie smiled and wondered why she could never think of anything to say.

"Does your mother expect you right home?" Cornelia asked.

"No," Ruthie said. Her mother had not been home since the fire.

"Do you think you could sit on the front steps with me for a while? My mother's still at the hospital. I have a key, but I'm afraid to go in the house by myself, do you know what I mean?"

"Yes," Ruthie said, "I know."

"I guess you know my daddy's real sick," Cornelia said.

Ruthie nodded.

Cornelia jumped up. "Would you like to play Monopoly?" she asked.

"Okay," Ruthie said.

Cornelia went into the house to get the game. She looked back at Ruthie apprehensively. "You won't go, will you? You'll stay to play the game?"

Ruthie smiled. Cornelia was really anxious. It was a good feeling to be needed by Cornelia. "I can stay till your mother comes home if you want."

"You can? Oh, thanks." Cornelia disappeared. In three seconds she was back on the porch with the game box. They took the board out and the markers. Ruthie sorted out the properties, and Cornelia divided the play money.

Cornelia sighed. She held the wad of five-hundred-dollar bills. "Oh, Ruthie! Look at all the money. What would you do if it was real?"

"I don't know. Buy things, I guess."

"I'd give it to my parents to pay my daddy's doctor bills. It costs an awful lot to be sick, Ruthie. We almost don't have any money left. I think we're poor now. I guess you don't know how that feels. It's just terrible."

"I sort of know," Ruthie whispered, but Cornelia didn't seem to hear her. The game started.

Cornelia bought a railroad and Ruthie bought a utility. They played for an hour until both girls owned several houses and hotels.

Cornelia got sort of nervous and kept looking up the road.

"What time does your mom come home?" Ruthie asked.

"She catches the four-o'clock bus, but sometimes it's late."

"Well, she'll probably come any minute. Do you want to put the game away?"

"Okay. I'm kind of tired of it. I think you won, Ruthie. You had more property."

They picked up the money and markers and put them neatly in the box.

"It's too bad Edgar has to move away," Ruthie said.

"He might get a pony."

"I know," Ruthie said. Then she was embarrassed. "I mean, I heard. I was walking behind you on the way home."

"It's hard to lose a friend," Cornelia said, looking down over the hill to where Edgar lived for three more days. "You know what it feels like? It feels like a blue spot in your stomach."

Suddenly the words burst out of Ruthie. "Honestly, I don't know what it feels like. You probably don't understand, Cornelia, you have so many friends—I can't think of anybody in the whole fifth grade that isn't your friend. But I—I've never lost a friend, because I've never had a friend."

Ruthie's face turned red. Where had the words come from? She hadn't meant to say them at all.

Cornelia stared at Ruthie. She was just about to speak

when she jumped up and ran down the driveway, screaming, "Mommy!"

Ruthie turned and saw Cornelia leap into her mother's open arms. Ruthie's chest ached at the sight and she put her hand on her heart to ease the pain. Mrs. Lee looked so pretty. She gave Cornelia a tight hug.

Cornelia had an arm around her mother's back as they walked up on the porch.

"Wasn't Ruthie nice to stay with me, Mommy? She won the Monopoly game."

Mrs. Lee patted Ruthie's shoulder. "Thank you, Ruthie."

Cornelia started to snicker, then burst out in a big giggle as she said, "Ruthie is my baby-sitter!"

Ruthie laughed too. Even Mrs. Lee laughed with the girls, though her eyes looked kind of red and tired. When they had stopped giggling, Ruthie ran off the porch, waving.

" 'Bye!" she said. She ran over the hills, all the way home. She felt exhilarated. Special! She had been giggling with Cornelia. Maybe Cornelia liked her a little! Maybe . . . was it possible? . . . Cornelia could be her friend?

Chapter Eleven

Ruthie became obsessed with the idea that if she could find the little turquoise stone that had fallen from Cornelia's ring, the Lees could sell it and pay Mr. Lee's doctor bills with the money.

She spent all her time searching for the stone in the vacant lot next to the Lees. Some days she looked wherever she had an inkling it might be. Other days she was very systematic, beginning at one corner and searching there, then walking around the edge of the lot and closing in on a circle till she was searching the middle.

Several times Cornelia or Mrs. Lee would look out a window and see Ruthie in the vacant lot. When they asked her if she had lost anything, Ruthie just said that she was looking for a brown toad she had seen jump in off the road. Once she said she was looking for a red bird's feather that she had seen fall as the bird flew over the lot. They seemed to accept her explanations. They would wave and walk away from the window.

Mr. Lee was home now, but he couldn't work. He had to stay in bed. And he had to have something that helped him breathe. The Lees seemed to get poorer and poorer. Cornelia brought only a sandwich for lunch now, and she said that her parents might have to sell their house. Ruthie felt terrible about that, and she thought, If I could just find that turquoise stone, the Lees would be rich again and everything would be all right.

One day in April Ruthie went to the lot, planning again on finding the stone. But a man and woman were there. The man had a spade and he was turning up the earth. Ruthie couldn't believe it. She assumed they were trespassers and ran to them, calling, "Stop! Stop! In the name of the law!"

The man put the spade down. He was becoming weary of digging anyhow.

The woman smiled sweetly at Ruthie. "What is it, dear? Did you used to play here? Is that what's bothering you?"

Ruthie stared at the overturned dirt. She tried to kick it back in place. "Get out of here. You'll lose the little

stone for good. What do you think you're doing here?"
she said.

The man tried to calm her down, but it didn't seem to
do any good. "Now, my dear girl, this lot belongs to us,
has for a long time. We're at war, you know. And the
only thing the wife and I can do to help is save the bacon
fat and raise a Victory garden. And that's what our lot's
going to be here, a Victory garden."

The woman winked at her husband. "What say if we
give the nice little girl a few rows to plant some seeds?"

He nodded.

"Would you like that, now?" the woman said to Ruthie.
"Have a little Victory garden right here in your old playing place. It'd be real patriotic. You could come by and
water it each day and watch it grow, eat the vegetables
when they're ripe. What do you think, dear?"

But Ruthie had her heart set on finding the turquoise,
and she wasn't thinking. She was crying, loudly. She was,
in fact, wailing. It was so loud, so very strange-sounding,
that Mrs. Lee and Cornelia heard it. They ran out of
their house, and when they saw it was Ruthie making the
awful racket, they ran to her and put their arms around
her.

The woman and man were upset. They told Mrs. Lee,
"We didn't touch her. We don't know what set her off,
just that she doesn't seem to like the idea of our Victory
garden."

Mrs. Lee nodded to them. "We'll take her home with
us and see what the trouble is. She has been spending a

great deal of time here lately, every day after school for a month or more. Don't worry, now. Go on with your digging and come by to visit before you leave today. I haven't seen you for so long." She smiled, then she and Cornelia led the wailing Ruthie to their house. They sat down on the porch.

"Cornelia, could you mix a package of Kool Aid? Ruthie might like a drink."

Ruthie's chest was moving up and down in great sobs. She felt so weighted and depressed. She seemed to be letting out tears that she had kept stored up for years. The whole front of her dress was soaked with them. Mrs. Lee patted her back, and Ruthie cried and cried.

Cornelia brought a glass of red Kool Aid and offered it to Ruthie. Ruthie looked up at Cornelia and tried to say something, but it just sounded like a blubber.

Mrs. Lee ran to get some Kleenex so Ruthie could blow her nose. Ruthie also wiped her eyes and she took a sip of the red drink. Then she felt better, but she also felt foolish for making such a fuss.

"Do you want to tell us, dear?" Mrs. Lee said.

Ruthie clearly did not want to tell them. But they had been so nice that she finally did tell them, talking and sniffling at the same time.

"I lied to you before," she said. "I wasn't looking for a toad that day you asked. But I did see one jump in from the road. And I wasn't looking for a red bird's feather that other day. But I had seen one fall, and when you asked me, I already had it in my pocket. I was looking for the little turquoise stone that fell from Cornelia's ring. I thought I could find it. Then you could sell the ring and be rich again. You could pay all the doctor bills, and wouldn't have to sell your house. Now they're making a garden and I'll never find it for you." Ruthie began to sob again, but this time, the sobs were quiet and sad-sounding.

Mrs. Lee and Cornelia looked at each other. Tears came to their eyes, too.

"Ruthie," Mrs. Lee said, "that is the most wonderful thing anyone has ever wanted to do for us. I don't know how many days I saw you searching in that lot. You tried so very hard to help us. You are a beautiful little girl."

Ruthie stopped crying when she heard the word *beautiful* and looked at Mrs. Lee.

"Ruthie, there's a wealth in you that you don't realize," Mrs. Lee said.

Ruthie shook her head. "Honestly, Mrs. Lee, we don't have any wealth. We're just as poor as can be."

Mrs. Lee smiled. "Well, darling, so are we. But we have a lot to be thankful for. Mr. Lee is over the worst. We know he is going to get better now, though it will take time."

"Will we still have to sell the house, Mommy?" Cornelia asked.

"Yes. To pay the bills. Your father won't be able to work for several months. He has a lot of healing to do. And, Ruthie dear, your thoughtfulness about trying to find the turquoise was very sweet. But I don't think the ring would sell for more than twenty-five dollars. I'm afraid our doctor bills are in the thousands."

"But aren't we lucky, Mommy, to have Ruthie for a friend?" Cornelia asked.

Mrs. Lee smiled, "Our very fine, very best, loyal friend, Ruthie Hickory."

Ruthie looked at Cornelia. Then she looked at Mrs. Lee. She wiped her eyes again, with her arm, and when her face emerged there was a gentle, ever-growing smile on it.

Chapter Twelve

From that day on, Ruthie and Cornelia walked to school and home from school together, every day. And they played together at recess and after school. Ruthie showed Cornelia her favorite place by the creek, where the wild violets grew. They had secrets. And they giggled. They were *best friends*.

One night Ruthie told her father that the Lees had sold their house.

"What are they going to do now?" he asked.

"They're going to buy a trailer with what's left over from the doctor bills. And they'll live in the trailer," Ruthie told him.

"Do they have a piece of land to keep it on?" he asked.

"I don't know, Daddy. Cornelia didn't say."

"You two are pretty thick lately," he said, and he was smiling.

"Daddy! I told you we were best friends!" Ruthie smiled too because she knew he was teasing her.

Mr. Hickory thought a bit, then said, "I have some flat land at the bottom of the hill, beside the road. Seems like it might be a good trailer site. I'll talk to Fred Lee about it."

Ruthie ran to her father and hugged him. "Oh, Daddy, would you? We can see that flat part from our place. We'd be practically next-door neighbors. That would be just perfect!"

The Lees were grateful to Ruthie's father for the use of his land. They sold their furniture, moved out of their house and into their trailer. It was hard to get used to the small space. They had to have a well dug for water, and they paid Mr. Hickory to build them an outdoor toilet. Mrs. Lee cooked with Sterno. At night they read by the light of kerosene lamps. It was like living in a different world.

At first it was a lark, something new and different. But soon the dreariness of it all began to drag them down. They found themselves losing their tempers with each other, and sometimes they spent sad, thoughtful evenings thinking about their comfortable house and how things used to be.

Mrs. Lee became upset because there wasn't much money to buy groceries. She had to buy day-old bread, and she tried to make interesting dinners without meat, dinners sometimes without practically anything. She even had more ration stamps and tokens than she could use because she didn't have enough money to buy the items. The Lees discovered the hard way that it was not easy to be poor.

Mrs. Lee took a job cleaning house on Saturdays, and she baby-sat whenever she got work in the evenings or on Sundays. Cornelia took care of Mr. Lee at these times. People from the Presbyterian Church brought them gifts of garden vegetables and homemade cakes. They got to know well the feeling of charity received, and though they did not like the feeling, they hungrily ate the food.

Some days Ruthie noticed that Mrs. Lee and Cornelia took to staring at Mr. Lee as if they were looking for, seaching for, a sign that he was well, a sign that he could work again and be responsible for his family. At other times, self-consciously, they did not look his way at all, as if he did not exist. Sometimes Mrs. Lee seemed to be thinking, Will we ever be the same again? Is something terrible, *permanent,* happening to us?

Ruthie watched them change, slowly, subtly. They tried not to change, she knew. But life was so different now. So hard.

Ruthie's mother came home the middle of May. She had stayed away almost a year. Ruthie did not recognize her. Her brown hair was dyed orange-red. She had taken the bus out from town and had noticed the trailer on her way up the hill. She was curious about it.

"Who's got the trailer on our land, Tommy?" she wanted to know. "Are you getting rental, or are you somebody's sucker again?"

Ruthie stared at her mother's beautiful red velveteen dress.

"I'll be getting paid when Fred Lee gets back to work," her father said.

Her mother's eyebrows just about flew off her head. "The Lees?" she screamed. "The big fancy Lees with their car and house and fancy ways?" Then she laughed. She really laughed hard, as though she hadn't had a good laugh in a long time. "If that isn't something. *Them* living in a run-down trailer on our land. And using an outhouse. Well, it sure is a pleasure to see those high and mighty people eat dust." She laughed some more, as if she'd never stop laughing. The sound would go on forever, Ruthie thought, past the trees, past the clouds to the stars.

"Where did you get those pretty clothes, Mother?" Ruthie asked.

Her mother looked down at her dress as if it were some old rag. "Oh, you can get them in the city."

Ruthie ran to her father and threw her arms around him. "Oh, Daddy, let's move to the city!" she said.

He brushed stiff strands of hair from her forehead. "You run along now, Ruthie. Go down and play with your best friend." He smiled at her. "Your ma and I got some talking to do."

Ruthie knew to go right away. She took off down the hill, running fast and singing loud so she wouldn't hear the loud words and the screaming.

The next morning, before she took the curlers out of her hair, Mrs. Hickory threw on her blue silk bathrobe and walked down to the Lee's trailer. She knocked at the door.

Mrs. Lee opened it. "Yes?" she said.

"I'm your landlord's wife," Mrs. Hickory said.

"Oh, Mrs. Hickory, I'm sorry. I didn't recognize you."

"It's my new hair color. Cinnamon red."

"Yes, that must be it," Mrs. Lee said.

"Well," Mrs. Hickory said, "I think the best thing is to be frank, don't you? I don't like to beat around the bush. So I'm going to just come out and tell you. I don't want my daughter Ruth associating with your daughter Cornelia. It's not a good mix, us being your landlords and all. If the time comes you don't pay your rent, the situation could get messy. Do you see what I mean?"

Mrs. Lee's face lost its color. She couldn't find any words. But she nodded and slowly closed the door.

Inside the trailer, Cornelia and Ruthie stood shaking. Mrs. Lee peeked out a window. "Thank heavens she didn't ask to come in. I don't know what she would have done. You girls better hurry on to school now. And try not to cry. Ruthie, I'm sorry, darling. You know we love you. But I guess you'd better not come here anymore."

Chapter Thirteen

On the way to school Cornelia wiped her eyes and looked at Ruthie.

"What are we going to do?" she said.

"Well," Ruthie said, "I've been thinking. You should always do what your mother says. Right?"

"I guess so," Cornelia said sadly.

"But I think my mother is a mistake. I think my father is really my mother. He's my mother and my father. I know it's confusing. It gives me a headache to think about it. But he's really the one who takes care of me. And I know he wants us to be friends."

"Does that mean we can still be friends?" Cornelia asked.

Ruthie sighed. "I don't know."

"Maybe if your mother doesn't find out?"

"I have a really terrible headache," Ruthie said. "Maybe she'll go away again."

"Where does she go?"

Ruthie cupped her hands around her mouth and whispered in Cornelia's ear. "Don't tell anyone. I just found out. She goes to the *city*."

At school, Mercy Berry and De De Colona were waiting by the fence for Ruthie and Cornelia. Ever since Cornelia had moved into the trailer, they waited by the fence to give the girls the "treatment."

"Here comes Corny and Hickory Stick," Mercy said, giggling.

"Boy, it sure smells like a couple of pigpens," De De said.

Ruthie and Cornelia walked on by as fast as they could. Sometimes Mercy would put a foot out and trip one of them. Ruthie didn't mind the name calling as much as Cornelia did. Ruthie was used to it. But for Cornelia, it was a brand-new, horrible thing.

In English lesson, Ruthie made a poem out of it, but she never showed it to the teacher. She just ripped it up and threw it away. She had written:

WILD VIOLETS

When They Called Her Corny

by Ruthie Hickory

They took her star out of the sky
And stomped on it.
It's a lot harder on her
Than it ever was on me
Because I have not made it
To the sky yet.

At lunch recess Mercy lured Ruthie and Cornelia around to the back of the school. She said she needed them for a Red Rover game. They were glad to be asked because no one picked them for games nowadays. They were even picked last for the spelling-bee teams.

At the back of the school a group of children were standing in a circle with their backs to the girls as though they were in a football huddle. Ruthie recognized De De Colona, Harry Tompkins, Grover Wilson, and some of the other fifth graders.

The signal must have been when Mercy called out, "Here they are!"

The whole group in the huddle turned around yelling and screaming and throwing things at Ruthie and Cornelia. The girls heard "Surprise!" and "A present for the pigpens!" as they got battered by wadded-up wax paper, an old carrot, apple cores, and old lunch bags. Somebody had aimed well at Cornelia, for she was hit directly in her left eye with an apple. It must have been thrown by Harry Tompkins because he got a funny look on his face when she screamed. The other children laughed and ran away, all except Ruthie and Cornelia and Harry, who was standing there looking funny.

Ruthie put her arm around Cornelia.

"Do you want to go to the nurse?" she asked.

Harry started to shake. "Are you going to tell? I didn't mean it. I still like you, Cornelia. It was Mercy's idea. We can team up on the other guys. Here, I'll gather up these apple cores and wax-paper bombs, and we'll attack them." He frantically began gathering up the garbage.

But Ruthie and Cornelia walked away.

On the way home from school Ruthie could see Cornelia's eye was all red and bloodshot in the white part. And the skin around the eye was turning navy blue.

"Does it hurt?" Ruthie asked.

Cornelia nodded yes. "I know my mother is going to ask about it. And I hate to see her cry. She doesn't know how mean everyone's been since we sold our house and got poor. I wonder now if anyone really liked me at all."

"They did, Cornelia. They still do, but that darned Mercy is so hateful. She turns everyone mean. They can't help it. They're under her mean power."

"And now your mother doesn't want us to be friends. I won't have any friends."

"I won't either."

"Can't you tell your father?" Cornelia asked, a desperate tone in her voice.

Ruthie bent down and picked up some small rocks. She threw them at the telephone pole.

She said, "Maybe we could just secretly walk to school and home together. She'd never come to school to check at recess. Some days after school I could meet you down at the creek and we could hunt for bugs and things and pick wild violets."

"Why don't you just tell your dad on her? He wants us to play together," Cornelia insisted.

Ruthie frowned. "I don't want to bother him. He might have an awful fight with her about it. She might just run off because of it."

"I thought you'd like that. I thought you wanted her to go away."

Ruthie shook her head. "I don't know what I want. She drives me crazy. I wish . . . I wish she was a regular mother. Like your mother, Cornelia. I wish she'd make me a lunch and fix my hair and give me a hug at bedtime. I've heard your mother say she loves you. My mother hasn't ever said that to me. She's not an ordinary mother at all. She's a crazy, wild, running-off sort of mother. But she's all I've got. So I just don't know. But I'll meet you at the creek today if you want. We could build a bridge across it. Would you like that?"

Cornelia smiled. "Should I bring anything?"

"Just some wood or a big rock if any's around your place, and wear old clothes in case we fall in."

The idea of the bridge and the creek and falling in started a giggle in both the girls, and soon they were running and hopping and hurrying home as fast as they could.

Chapter Fourteen

Mr. Hickory noticed there were an awful lot of men prowling around the land adjacent to his, the land on the other side of the creek. There were surveyors, too, measuring the land and checking on property lines.

He wondered what was going on. And he heard some rumors about it. First he heard it was going to be the site of a big rodeo; then it was to be a warehouse, then an army post, an airplane-spotter site, and a chicken farm. It turned out that it wasn't to be any of those things. It was to be a government defense plant. They were going to build a factory that made small arms, like rifles and pistols, for the war.

The whole community was talking about it. They said it would be a real boon for the area. There would be lots of jobs for both men and women. And they would be patriotic jobs, so everyone could do his bit for the war effort.

Ruthie's mother said she was going to kill herself when she found out the whopping amount the government had paid for the property.

"I heard it was over a hundred thousand dollars," she said. "Why can't we have any luck like that? What's the matter with our side of the creek? We could have been on easy street." She really got depressed about it and moped around for days.

Mr. Hickory kept telling her she heard wrong, that the government hadn't paid anywhere near that figure for the land. But once she'd heard a hundred thousand dollars mentioned, she just couldn't get the money out of her head. And she talked about it all the time, saying they had just missed out on it, when really their land had not been considered at all.

But several weeks later two men in business suits came to talk to Ruthie's father. He wouldn't say what the talk was about, and Mrs. Hickory was beside herself thinking about it. She must have asked him a million questions, but all he would say was, "I'll discuss it with you if anything ever comes of it. We don't want to get our hopes up for nothing."

She swore she was going to die if he didn't tell her. But he didn't tell her for several weeks and she managed to stay alive.

He finally announced that he was ready to discuss it one evening at supper.

"Ruthie," he said, "something's come up that I want your permission on."

"What? What is it?" she said.

"Well, some gentlemen have been around asking about some land I own."

Mrs. Hickory nearly fell off her chair when she heard that.

"And I have to talk to you before I sell."

Ruthie looked puzzled and didn't know what to say.

"Sell it!" her mother said. "Don't fool around. Sell it before they change their mind." She was practically screaming.

"Now calm down," Mr. Hickory said. "Ruthie, they're interested in about two acres down by the creek. It's the spot where you like to play. They need more parking space for the defense plant, and they're going to build a bridge over the creek and put a parking space on two acres of our land there. I said I'd have to talk to you first. You wouldn't be able to go down there to play anymore. But, on the other hand, we'd get a little money to put in the bank, and when you're ready to go to college, why, you could go. You don't have to decide tonight. You think about it. I told them I'd give you time to think about it. I know you love it down by the creek."

Mrs. Hickory stood up in disgust. "Now I know you're crazy. You are crazy, crazy, crazy."

Ruthie felt all funny inside. So many things to think about. Her mind was whirling, but she somehow calmed it down. She thought carefully, and then she spoke.

"Daddy, you can sell my place by the creek. Some people are dying in the war. Everybody's making sacrifices. The creek will be mine."

Ruthie's mother shouted "Hallelujah!" and danced around in circles. "Wait till your sister Lenore hears about this. She can keep her old fruitcake now. How much are we going to get, Tommy?" she asked. "Ten thousand?"

Mr. Hickory smiled. "No, not ten thousand, but it won't be anything to sneeze at."

Three weeks later Mr. Hickory received payment for the land. He put it all into a savings account at a local bank.

That night, Mrs. Hickory said, "I need fifty dollars, Tommy. I'm going shopping tomorrow."

"I don't have fifty dollars," he said.

"Well, where is it? I know you got the check. What's the sense of having money if you can't spend it?" she argued.

"It's in the bank, and that's where it's going to stay. I like the feeling of knowing it's there."

"But we need so much. Let's just spend a little. Let's

78

get a washing machine and a decent stove and refrigerator. You should have a car, Tommy. And we could all of us use a new outfit of clothes."

"See," he said, "you just spent it in one sentence."

"Well," she sulked, "you're being mean not to improve us a little. Everyone is expecting us to get new things. Clothes and furniture and stuff."

But Mr. Hickory was stubborn about it. He said he would not let her spend a dime of it. Well, maybe just a couple extra dollars a week for food, but that was all. They would just have to get on the way they had gotten on before. He was going to be a man with money in the bank, and that was that.

Chapter Fifteen

By the beginning of August life was very rosy for Ruthie Hickory. Although no evidence of money showed by any outward appearance, Ruthie, like her father, had the good feeling of knowing it was there if they needed it. She developed more self-confidence, laughed more, and her mouth more easily turned to smiles. And her mother was so busy plotting how to get hold of the money that she forgot she had forbidden Cornelia and Ruthie to play. Sometimes, absentmindedly, she would say, "Why don't you go see your little friend at the trailer today?" or "Why don't you and Cornelia walk over to the defense plant and see how it's coming along?"

Mrs. Hickory made a new plan every day for a way to get hold of some of the money. Each day the plan failed when Mr. Hickory said no, but she never stopped trying. The next day she'd wake up with a new plan. It seemed as if she'd never go away, not as long as the money was there like a magnet for her.

So Ruthie and Cornelia had a wonderful summer together, playing every day. Ruthie thought, Having a friend is the most wonderful feeling in the world.

And life was getting brighter for Cornelia too. Her father was feeling better, and he was up and about, puttering around the trailer, taking walks up and down the road to gain his strength. Mrs. Lee sang a lot. Yes, life was pretty fine for the Lees too. Mr. Lee even took a job one day repairing some wiring in a house on the street where they used to live. Cornelia confided to Ruthie that soon everything would be like old times for her family because both her mother and father had been promised jobs when the defense plant opened.

But suddenly one night, in the midst of all her happiness, Ruthie's world fell apart. She heard her father tell her mother that he had enlisted in the army. He was going to be a soldier!

It was bedtime and they were talking in the loft, thinking she was asleep. Actually she had been asleep, but the talking woke her up.

She was a little groggy but she heard her father say, "I couldn't stand waiting around to be drafted. Doing nothing is terrible. I want to get into the action. So I joined up today."

"You're going off to war!" her mother said. "Oh, Tommy, that's so exciting. I can't wait to see your uniform. You'll be the handsomest soldier!"

"Look, it wouldn't be right for me to sit around waiting to be called. I'm in shape and I want to help win the war. I know we can."

"Listen, Tommy, all I ask is, don't let me stay behind. I want to follow you around the camps till you go overseas. I could live in the town near your base. Lots of girls do that. Being around an army base sounds so exciting. We could go dancing when you get a pass. What do you say, Tommy? Take me with you?" Mrs. Hickory begged.

Ruthie slid down in the sheets till even her eyes were covered. But she could still hear her father's voice.

"That might be fun at that," he said. Then they started laughing together about it and making plans.

Ruthie's head felt as if it had grown as big as a house. She quietly slipped out of bed and got dressed. Her heart was pounding so loudly she thought for sure they would hear it. But *they* were have too much fun with their plans for leaving *her*. And no one heard. They didn't even hear the door close when she went out into the night.

The first thing that struck her was the very blackness of it all. Not just the sky was black. The air was black,

82

and it closed in around her and touched her with its black coolness. She wished she had grabbed a sweater on the way out. She clutched her elbows and shivered. Where to go? What to do? Now they'd be sorry. She'd see to that.

She didn't know which way to go, and she stumbled. She finally decided to wander down near the Lees' trailer. She would feel safe there. Then, when it got light, she could hide in the woods.

She slowly made her way down the dirt road to the Lees'. She sat on the stoop outside their door to wait out the night. She was glad she had thought of them. She did feel safer sitting on their stoop, thinking of them sleeping just inside the door.

But the night was long, and the thoughts inside her head were painful. Tears came out of her eyes and moved down her face. They were hot tears and they warmed her skin. "How could they both leave me?" her heart cried out. "How could they not give a care about me? How could they laugh about it? How could they?"

At the beginning of dawn, she crept away to the woods, wondering when they would discover she was gone, wondering what they would do about it.

It wasn't long before she heard her name being called. The wind carried the sound down to her.

"Ruthie!"

It went on by her, through the trees, into the deep middle of the woods. Her father called again and again. But she didn't answer. She crouched low by the trunk of a great oak tree. A chipmunk scurried along on his morning walk, close enough to touch.

"Ruthie! Where are you?" her father called.

She took a twig and carved her name in the moss at the base of the tree.

"Ruthie!"

The tears came again, exploding out of her eyes. She could not even see through them. The chipmunk blurred till he looked as big as a dog. Finally the calling stopped. She walked deeper into the woods.

There was a nice grassy place she had never seen before. She lay down and curled up in it. She made pictures with the leaves against the sky. She rolled over and watched ants crawl through the thick mat of grass. Then she became hungry and tired at the same time and fell to napping, warmed by a patch of morning sun.

She woke up, not tired anymore, but still hungry. Once she thought, If I could get to the city, that's where I'd go. The afternoon bore on, the time going as slow as thick molasses. She wondered what was happening. Nothing was happening in the woods, that was for sure. Perhaps they had given up already and would leave her to live in the woods forever. She found some beautiful purple wild flowers but decided not to pick them. "There's no one to give them too," she told the tree.

When it got dark, she heard the fire sirens screaming, and it gave her a chill. Then the calling came again.

"Ruthie! Ruthie!"

Different voices. Men's voices. Many voices. Lights

flashing. She listened and watched, fascinated. When it all got quiet again, several hours later, she crept back to the Lees' trailer and sat on their stoop.

Fireflies put on a show for her. She heard an owl hoot in the woods. She heard Mr. Lee snoring in the trailer. That was a good sound. Her stomach ached. That was bad. She remembered the Victory garden on the lot by Cornelia's old house. Near daybreak she went to it and "borrowed" two tomatoes, a carrot, and a scallion. She took one last look back at the ground, thinking she had seen the turquoise. She touched the soft blue something she had seen. Part of a robin's egg shell. The sun was coming up, so she ran for cover in the woods.

She hungrily ate the vegetables. Now the horrible realization came upon her that she could live indefinitely in the woods, stealing at night from the Victory garden. She thought she might in some small way be in the same league as Benedict Arnold. Now they wouldn't have to find her till the snows came and she froze to death. She could live like the wild animals, sleeping in the day, prowling for food at night. It was not what she wanted at all, she decided. She wanted the nice part of summer back again —her mother and father at home, and her friend Cornelia to play with.

I wonder if Cornelia can guess where I am, she thought, and then she slept.

Chapter Sixteen

When she woke up in the afternoon of her second day in the woods, she broke up twigs and built a small log house from them. "Big enough for you, chipmunk," she said. And suddenly the tears came again. She cried and sobbed and moaned. And no one heard. The ants kept crawling through the thick grass. The owl slept on in a high branch of the tree. The chipmunk stayed in his hole.

The night again brought sirens and lights flashing. Her name was called, more desperately. She heard a loudspeaker blaring. It sounded like a woman's voice. Was it her mother? Or Mrs. Lee? She couldn't tell. The sound was so distorted.

"Ruthie," it said, "if you are in the woods, don't go near the creek. We just heard today one of your little friends from school went to the swimming pool and has caught polio. Don't go near the creek, Ruthie. Please come home. Cornelia wants you to come home. Please come home." Ruthie decided it was Mrs. Lee. She guessed her mother wouldn't bother.

As the sound of the searchers got closer to her, she went farther into the woods until she had gone so far that she walked out into an open space. The woods were long! Miles long. How far had she walked? Was she lost now, really lost? She ran back into the woods, her haven, and hid under a bush. She shook until she fell asleep there.

She fidgeted in her sleep and dreamed her father had found her. He tried to pick her up and take her home, but she fought him and got away. He caught her again, saying, "Why are you fighting me? I'm your father." She dreamed she pounded on his chest with her fists, yelling, "Because, you dumb man, you're going to be a soldier. You're running off from me just like she always runs off. I already gave up my place at the creek. *I can't give up you.*"

She woke to a foggy morning. Her third day. The thick white mist clung to the bushes and trees, even clung to her. Her clothes were damp. Her insides were all chilled, and she felt as though she were catching cold.

Her throat was sore. She stood up and tried to get her bearings, but with the foggy mist she could see only a few feet in front of her. She was a little scared because the night before she had come out into an open clearing, the end of the woods. She knew it was far from home. The woods were what connected her with home. She had to find her way back through them.

She started walking through the fog, holding on to bushes, looking for some sort of trail that was not there. She walked for several hours. She tried to walk in a straight line, but sometimes she had the feeling she was passing a tree that she had passed before.

When the fog cleared up she didn't know where she was. The day was dark and gloomy. She felt one raindrop. And then she felt many. What do the animals do when it rains? she wondered.

She looked up and saw a white bolt of lightning flash erratically across the sky. *Boom!* The thunder resounded in her ears. She shivered and looked up at all the trees protecting her. And she knew she was right where she shouldn't be in a storm. "Don't go under a tree," her teacher always said. But everywhere she looked there were trees.

She sat down and hugged her knees. The lightning flashed around her. She put her hands over her ears and closed her eyes. *Boom! Boom!* the thunder sounded. She heard a loud *slit*. A tree not far from her had been sliced in two. One side of it crashed down into a thicket of brambles. She felt like running. Her throat was really sore now and her forehead hot. The rain was falling fast and gushing into streamlets around her feet. She stood up so she wouldn't be sitting in a pool of water. She balanced herself against a tree, because she was slightly dizzy now.

The water, she noticed, was going in one direction, down a small slope she was on. Vaguely, it reminded her of the creek. The creek! Perhaps the rain was flowing to the creek. She could follow the streamlets, and if they led to the creek she could surely find her way home.

The slope turned to mud. Her feet slipped and she slid on her bottom. She tried to grab at grasses, but nothing stopped her. She slid faster, as fast as the slide at the picnic grounds. At the bottom of the slope, she slid right into the creek. She stood up, now very wet. The creek rushed past her ankles. It seemed to be in such a hurry. She looked up the creek. She looked down the creek. Which direction was home?

She thought about her special place at the creek, which she had given up for the defense plant. She tried to remember how the creek flowed when she searched for polliwogs. And then she saw it flowing in her mind as if she were at the spot itself. Now she knew. She had to walk against the flow to get home.

There was no walking beside the creek here with its slippery, muddy banks, so she walked right in the water, trying not to step on the big, slick rocks. Farther on, she was able to walk along beside it in thick moss, but there came some more times when she simply had to walk in the water if she was going to find her way home.

Getting home was all she could think about now. Her throat ached all the way to her ears. She just wanted to get home. It was the only thing in her head.

She had to stop and rest. The rain was still coming down, but not as fast. She licked her lips and drank in the rainwater. It tasted good. She thought, I wonder who it is at school that got polio? She opened up her mouth to the rain and drank some more raindrops. Then she stood up, unsteadily, and began walking again, against the flow of the creek.

"I'll do it their way," she told the rushing water. "It's dumb to run away from something. The army needs my dad. And he needs my mother near the base to go dancing with. I can get along fine. I can cook a little. I can go to sixth grade. If I really get scared, I can go sit on the Lees' stoop. I'm eleven and a half. I can get on just fine. I'll put a star in the window. And when my daddy comes home from the war, we'll all be a family again. I can do it." The only thing she doubted was whether she could get home to tell them how sorry she was for running away.

The bushes and trees started dancing in front of her, and the creek played tricks with her eyes. Or were her eyes playing the tricks? She felt so dizzy.

Suddenly a big dark shadow loomed up on the edge of the creek. It was a man.

She rubbed her eyes and looked around. She was here! She saw the partially completed walls of the defense plant. She saw the beginnings of a bridge across her place on the creek.

Would he think she was a spy? A German or Japanese saboteur? She hoped he could see that she was just a little girl.

He seemed to know because he said, "You took a bad fall in the creek. What are you doing down here?"

Ruthie said, "I'm looking for the little girl that's lost." She didn't want to be rescued now. She knew she could make it, and she wanted to go home on her own, just as she had left.

Pure determination drove her up over the hill. There was the barn house. Her home. She didn't know what she was going to say. She opened the door and walked in, then she leaned back against the door so she wouldn't fall down. The room was going around in whirling circles.

"I'm home," she called.

Two forms that looked like her father came out from the kitchen. She was seeing double again. He ran to her and grabbed at her, hugging her and clinging to her.

"I'm getting you all wet," she said. "I'm sorry. About running away. It was a bad thing to do. I'm sorry I was so awful. I'll never do it again. I want you to be a soldier, Daddy, and I want her to go with you. I really want it that way."

Every muscle in her legs ached. And not just her legs. She ached all over, her arms, and just everywhere. Sweat came out of her forehead, and it was hard to distinguish it from the rest of her wetness.

Her father was practically speechless, but he managed to say, "Ruthie, you look sick. How do you feel?"

When her father said "feel," he stretched it out into a long, wavering word. Colorless little beads of water were moving from her father's eyes down his cheeks and dripping off his unshaved chin.

Ruthie reached out to touch her father's face. "I feel fine," she said. She stumbled toward him, and then she fainted.

Chapter Seventeen

Mr. Hickory put dry clothes on her and laid her on the couch. Then he ran to the nearest house that had a telephone and called a doctor.

Ruthie was very sick for two days. On the third day she felt better and sat up on the couch. She picked up the local weekly paper (the Blab Sheet everyone called it), because she saw her picture on the front page. The head-line said: "TRI-COUNTY SEARCH ENDED—GIRL COMES HOME ON HER OWN." Under her picture the caption said: "Sick from dehydration, overexposure, and the common cold." The article began, "A little girl who didn't want to see her daddy go to war came home today."

Ruthie threw the paper on the floor. "That isn't how it was at all!" she said.

Her mother came into the room, filing her nails with an emery board. "What is it? What's wrong now?"

Ruthie pointed to the paper. "That," she said. "Just wait till the kids at school see that. I can just hear Mercy Berry now. 'Does the little bitsy girlie hate to see her daddy-waddy go off to war?' She'll never let me hear the end of it."

Her mother reached down and brushed the stiff hair from Ruthie's forehead. "That straw!" she said. "Didn't you hear that the Berry girl was up to the swimming pool this summer and caught polio? Lookie here, I broke off my longest nail!"

"Not Mercy!" Ruthie said. And strangely enough, even though Mercy had never been her friend, Ruthie felt terrible. She lay down to rest again and to think about Mercy. She closed her eyes.

Ruthie dreaded the time that she knew was coming, the time when her father decided it was time to have a talk with her. She wanted to avoid the time or somehow keep putting it off. She knew it was all well and good that her father was glad she had come home, but she also knew that sometime, soon, she would get a good talking-to for running away.

She was right. A good talking-to was just what her father had in mind. If she had not suffered enough from overexposure and dehydration, he probably would have given her a good spanking, too.

She didn't know why he had to talk with her. She already felt bad enough. She had delayed his physical examination and Army tests. She felt as bad as the people with loose lips that sank ships. "Loose lips sink ships," was a warning not to give away information, for an enemy agent might be listening.

Her father spent a lot of time telling her what a bad thing she had done, how much trouble and anxiety she had caused, how many fire companies had been all over the place looking for her.

She nodded, agreeing with him that she had acted quite badly.

"Besides, it was all so foolish," he said. "Where is your head to think we'd leave you home to shift for yourself? I told you once if I ever went to war, you'd be taken good care of. Did you think I'd forget about you?"

Ruthie shrugged her shoulders.

Mr. Hickory went on. "My plan for you was to take you up to Utica to live with your Aunt Lenore till I got back from the war. You always liked her, what you saw of her, and she said she'd love to have you. Uncle Bob will be there, too. He couldn't get in the Army with those flat feet. Cousin Thomas drives a car now and spends his time with his high-school friends. Why, Aunt Lenore can't wait for you. She kept saying on the telephone,

'When do I get her? I can't wait!' "

"She is nice," Ruthie whispered.

"Sure she is. You didn't think I'd leave you with your mother, did you? She means well, but I'd always worry that she'd decide to run off or something on you. That's why, when she wanted to stay by my base, I said okay, because you were going to be having a fine time in Utica at your Aunt Lenore's."

"Oh," Ruthie said softly. "I didn't know."

Mrs. Hickory walked into the room. Nobody said anything.

"I heard that," she said, looking at her husband.

Ruthie slouched down on the couch and closed her eyes.

"You can quit playing possum, Ruthie, because there is some talking we have to do here tonight to get the record straight," her mother said.

Ruthie slowly opened her left eye, then her right one.

Her mother stood up straight and looked at both Ruthie and her husband. "I seem to be regarded as a no-account, as a lousy mother and who knows what else," she said.

Ruthie was so scared she held her breath.

"Well, I figure I got one life to lead," her mother said, "and I'm leading it."

The room was so quiet. Ruthie looked at her father, hoping he would say something. He didn't. Ruthie tried to think of something to say herself. Finally, she sat up and reached for her mother's hand. "I always liked you anyhow," Ruthie said.

Mrs. Hickory moved her hand out of Ruthie's reach. "For heaven's sake, will you two stop staring at me? You make me feel like I suddenly became bald or something. C'mon, Tommy, let's show Ruthie that new dance step, the lindy, the one I taught you while she was gone."

Ruthie watched her mother coax her father to dance. She set her mouth and stubbornly refused to believe her father could have been dancing one second while she was gone. She's saying that to get my goat, Ruthie thought, and I just won't let her.

What was it her Aunt Lenore had told her father? "When do I get her? I can't wait!" Ruthie thought of that.

Chapter Eighteen

Cornelia and Mrs. Lee had been planning a little farewell party for Ruthie for several days. It wasn't going to be the kind of party where lots of people are invited. It was just going to be the Lee family and Ruthie. Mrs. Lee had been up to Mrs. Perkin's house, on her old street, making cookies that you have to leave in the refrigerator overnight before they can be sliced and baked. She wasn't able to bake in the trailer. Overnight cookies were Cornelia's favorite and her request for the party.

They were also planning to have wild raspberries with milk. Cornelia had picked the berries, and she had just about died to be not able to eat any when she was picking. But she did want to be sure there were enough raspberries.

The last thing on the party menu would be orangeade. Mrs. Lee had squeezed about six oranges into the bottom of her big glass pitcher. Then she'd added two spoons of lemon juice and a little sugar, and filled the pitcher with cold water and stirred it. Cornelia and Ruthie had always loved Mrs. Lee's orangeade. They liked it much better than lemonade or iced tea.

"You'd better get dressed now," Mrs. Lee told Cornelia. "It's almost time."

Cornelia pulled the blue curtain for privacy. She took off her one-piece sunsuit and hung it on a hook. Then she took a washrag and washed her face and under her arms. She held her arms up and studied her armpits in the mirror. I'll have to start shaving soon, she thought.

Then she dried herself and put the puffy pink dress from her ninth birthday party over her undershirt and pants. She had grown since then, and her mother had had to let the hem down two inches. In another week she would be celebrating her tenth birthday. There would be no birthday party or party dress this year, and there would be no Ruthie. Of course, she would still celebrate with her parents.

"I see Ruthie coming," Mrs. Lee called, "and I wanted to do your pigtails again."

"I'm hurrying," Cornelia said, trying to button the back of her dress but only fastening the two buttons at her waist. She pushed aside the curtain and handed the hairbrush to her mother. "Quick," she said.

"I'll be quick if you don't scream at the knots," Mrs. Lee said.

Cornelia grimaced. There was a knock at the trailer door.

"Come in, Ruthie!" they both called. Ruthie opened the door. She was wearing a new light-green dress with smocking on the blouse and new Mary Jane shoes.

"You look so pretty," Cornelia said, "and I'm not dressed yet."

Ruthie held a handful of wild flowers. She gave them to Mrs. Lee. "I picked them for you," she said.

Mrs. Lee finished Cornelia's hair, then put the flowers in a water glass and placed them in the center of the table. "They are the prettiest things," she told Ruthie. "Getting flowers is like getting a big hug."

"Well, I'll do that too," Ruthie said, hugging Mrs. Lee.

"Oh, Ruthie, we are going to miss you," Mrs. Lee said. "Now you two go outside and play awhile. Then, when Daddy comes, we'll eat."

"Ruthie, will you finish buttoning me?" Cornelia said.

"Shall I tie your sash, too?" Ruthie asked.

"Please."

Then the girls went outside and Ruthie told Cornelia that her new dress and shoes were for the trip to Utica the next day but that her father had said this day was special, so she could wear them to the Lee party.

"It's a pretty dress," Cornelia said.

"It's new. Nobody else ever wore it but me!" Ruthie said. "My father says Aunt Lenore will be wanting to dress me in clothes like this all the time. He says she sews her own clothes and she'll want to sew mine and she's already started to knit me a red sweater. And she's going to make a white bedspread and fluffy white curtains for my room. I'll have my own room, did I tell you? And a real bed. And Uncle Bob is starting to make me a doll-house with tiny furniture and flowered wallpaper on the walls. He has a new defense job."

"Oh," Cornelia said dreamily.

"I can't believe it's happening to me! And my mother was so silly this morning, laughing and teasing me. She said Aunt Lenore will spend half the day asking if I've had a bowel movement, and if I don't she'll make me eat fruitcake morning, noon, and night!"

"That would be awful," Cornelia said, giggling.

"I know," Ruthie said. "My mother isn't always . . . sometimes she's, you know . . . um . . . sort of nice."

"I bet your father will be the handsomest soldier in the war. I wish my father could be a soldier. He's too old."

"He doesn't look old."

"He's thirty-six."

"Oh."

"Probably by next summer we'll be starting to build our new house. Ruthie, I hate to think of being at Cranberry without you."

"You'll have Mrs. Franklin, the school principal. She won't stand for anybody being mean to you. You know it, Cornelia. Mrs. Franklin never stands for that."

"I hear Mercy will be in a wheelchair. Are you sure my sash is tied?" Cornelia asked.

"Oh, it's come loose," Ruthie said, tying it again. "I'm not very good at this."

Mr. Lee came home and said hello to the girls. He went into the trailer, and soon Mrs. Lee was calling for them to come in and eat. It was kind of crowded with four at the little table, but they all enjoyed the cookies and berries and orangeade.

"How long a drive is it to Utica?" Mr. Lee asked.

"I don't know," Ruthie said. "It will be a long bus ride. There are stops and things."

"I would think three hours," Mrs. Lee said.

"Maybe when we get a car again," Mr. Lee said, "we could find out for sure."

Cornelia and Ruthie looked at each other.

"I want to get another Ford," Mr. Lee said, lost in a dream of the past.

"We'll have another Ford," Mrs. Lee assured him. "We'll have lots of Fords in our lifetime."

Mr. Lee sighed, unconvinced.

"It wouldn't do any good now, anyhow, with gas rationing," Mrs. Lee said. "Although, if I know you, you'd be happy to just look at it or sit in it without moving."

Mr. Lee laughed then, as if pleased at this vision of himself being revealed.

"Let's go outside, Ruthie," Cornelia said.

As they jumped off the trailer stoop, Cornelia said, "My sash is untied again!"

"Oh," Ruthie said. "Let me tie it real tight." She took the sash and pulled. "Scream if I squeeze you."

"Done?" Cornelia said.

Ruthie didn't answer.

"Ruthie? Are you done tying my bow?" Cornelia repeated. "What are you doing?"

Ruthie untied the bow she had just tied. She brought one end of the sash around to show Cornelia. "Look at this bump in the material. It feels like a pebble inside your sash. See?"

"How could a pebble get in there? I only wear it for dress-up."

"Maybe it isn't a pebble," Ruthie said, thinking. "Let's ask your mother to get it out."

They ran to Mrs. Lee. Ruthie showed her the little bump in Cornelia's sash.

"How could a pebble get in my sash?" Cornelia asked her mother.

"I guess an opening in the seam. Seems I do recall sewing up such an opening in this sash once," Mrs. Lee said.

"Can you take it out?" Ruthie asked, her fingers crossed.

"Why are your fingers crossed, Ruthie?" Cornelia asked.

"Because," Ruthie said, but she wouldn't tell the reason.

Mrs. Lee got her scissors. "I'll split the seam here," she said, "and get the little dickens out of there."

In a matter of seconds, Ruthie and Cornelia and Mr. and Mrs. Lee were all staring at what had been in Cornelia's party-dress sash.

"Why, it's the little turquoise stone from your ring, Cornelia!" Mrs. Lee said.

"Ruthie, you found it!" Cornelia said.

"To think how many times I've washed and ironed this without noticing. I must have pushed the little turquoise around no end," Mrs. Lee said. "Once I told you it would turn up. I gave up thinking that long ago."

"It must have caught in the open seam when we were playing games at my birthday party," Cornelia said.

Ruthie couldn't say anything. Not anything! She had dreamed of finding the turquoise and now it had happened. She thought how strange life was. She had become friends with Cornelia because of the turquoise. And now she had found it on the last day she would see Cornelia for a long, long time. Well, I won't think about it, Ruthie told herself. I know I'll like it at Aunt Lenore's, but I also know I'll turn up around these parts again someday. Just like the little turquoise turned up, she thought.

Soon Ruthie and Cornelia were outside the trailer, making plans to write to each other.